Star's Turn

Linda Newbery

Illustrated by Peter Bailey

CORGI PUPS

To the children of Courtlands School, Plymouth

STAR'S TURN
A CORGI PUPS BOOK : 0 552 546550

First publication in Great Britain

PRINTING HISTORY
Corgi Pups edition published 1999

Set in 18/25pt Bembo Schoolbook by
Phoenix Typesetting, Ilkley, West Yorkshire.

Corgi Pups Books are published by Transworld Publishers,
61-63 Uxbridge Road, London W5 5SA,
a division of The Random House Group Ltd,
in Australia by Random House Australia (Pty) Ltd,
20 Alfred Street, Milsons Point, Sydney, NSW 2061, Australia,
in New Zealand by Random House New Zealand Ltd,
18 Poland Road, Glenfield, Auckland 10, New Zealand
and in South Africa by Random House (Pty) Ltd,
Endulini, 5a Jubilee Road, Parktown 2193, South Africa.

Made and printed in Great Britain by
Cox & Wyman Ltd, Reading, Berkshire.

Contents

Series reading consultant: Prue Goodwin,
Reading and Language Information Centre,
University of Reading

Chapter One

Star and Moon were best
friends. They lived together in a
small paddock, grazing side by
side.

Moon's real name was Precious
Moonstone of the Orient. He
was pure white, with a long
flowing mane and tail and a
silky coat. His great-great-
grandfather was a famous
racehorse.

Star's name was just Star. He had a scruffy grey coat, long ears and a tassel of a tail, and he was rather plain. He didn't know who his relations were, or even whether he had any relations at all.

In summer, Moon's owner
would take him into the stable
yard, where she would wash and
groom and polish him until he
gleamed like the new moon.
She brushed and plaited his
mane and tail and oiled his
hooves to make them shine.

Then she led him up the ramp of a smart horsebox and drove him away to a big horse show. Moon spent the whole summer winning prizes. In Moon's owner's house, the mantelpiece was loaded with cups and trophies and the walls were decorated with coloured rosettes.

All Moon's.

Star had never won a rosette in his life. Not one. He hardly ever left the paddock. But he liked listening to Moon. In the long summer evenings, when Moon stayed outside, they would lie on

the grass side by side. Moon told
Star about the grand shows he
had been to, the other beautiful
horses he had seen, and the
important people who presented
the prizes.

Sometimes, Star dreamed that
it was *his* turn – just once – to
go to a big show. He would be
admired by everyone, and he
would come home with a shiny
trophy of his own. But when he

looked at his reflection in the pond, he had to admit that he was very shaggy and not at all beautiful. His reflection stared back at him, with its long hairy ears, long bristly whiskers and long sad face. His legs were spindly and he had bulgy knees.

No-one would ever choose him to win a trophy. Nor a rosette. Not even for fourth or fifth or sixth prize.

He pawed the water with his front hoof and broke up his reflection into ripples. It was no use dreaming. He would never be as beautiful or as famous as Moon.

When winter came, Star spent most of his time alone in the paddock. It was too cold for Moon to be outside at night. Moon slept in a warm stable with a deep bed of straw. His coat was clipped and he wore a blue rug with red binding. In the

daytime, if it wasn't too cold, he
wore a waterproof outdoor rug
and spent a few hours in the
paddock with Star. But always,
before dark, his owner came to
take him back to his stable.

"I wouldn't mind," Moon said
to Star, "if you shared my stable
with me. It's big enough for two.
It must be cold out here at night
and you haven't got a rug like I
have. There are good things to
eat in there, too — oats, barley,
sometimes a hot mash."

17

When Moon's owner came to collect him, Star went up to the gate too. He tried to push his nose through. He tried to follow Moon into the stable yard.

"No, not you, Star," Moon's owner said. "You're staying out."

And she pushed him back and bolted the gate. When she had led Moon away to his clean straw bed and his feed of oats, she threw some hay over the fence for Star. He tried to eat it without trampling it into the mud.

The winter nights were long and lonely. When the east wind blew and the cold rain lashed, Star sheltered by the clump of trees in the corner. He stood in the mud, head down, tail to the

wind, and he dreamed of
warmer days and lush grass.
Sometimes Moon would neigh
to him from the comfort of his
stable, and Star would bray an
answer.

"Soon it will be Christmas," Star thought to himself, "and then it won't be long to wait for spring. And then Moon will be here and we can graze together in the sunshine."

He tried not to think of all the cold lonely nights he would have to spend before the days grew warmer and longer. He shivered, and nibbled at a damp wisp of hay to keep his spirits up.

Chapter Two

In the village hall, children were rehearsing a play. The two teachers from the junior school had brought the children in for their first practice on the stage.

At the end, when all the
children had gone home, Mr
Scott and Miss Kitaj tidied up.
Miss Kitaj noticed that Mr Scott
looked a bit gloomy.

"What's the matter?" she asked. "It went well, didn't it, for the first time?"

"Mmm. Apart from Darren Daykins bringing his gerbil and losing it under the stage," Mr Scott said.

"Well, yes. And apart from Marianne Mossop having a sore throat and not being able to say a single word," Miss Kitaj added.

"And apart from Simon Stern getting hiccups behind the curtain and sending everyone on stage into a fit of giggles," Mr Scott said.

"Yes, but you've got to *expect* things like that to happen," Miss Kitaj said. "It was only the first proper run-through." She fished a small one-eared teddy bear from behind a radiator. She wondered whether one of the children had brought it, or whether it had been left over from the last jumble sale. "But *apart* from those things, it went well, didn't it?" she said. "All the children were here. They knew their lines — well, most of them. Everyone knew when to come on."

Mr Scott sighed.

"Yes, it was all right," he said.

"Then what's the matter?"
Miss Kitaj asked.

"I want it to be *better* than all right," Mr Scott said. "All right isn't good enough. There's something missing. We need an extra something."

"An extra what?" asked Miss Kitaj.

Mr Scott sighed again.

"I don't know," he said. "I've been trying to think, but I just don't know."

Chapter Three

On a cold grey Saturday
afternoon, two children walked
along the lane and stood
peeping over the hedge at Star
and Moon. Apart from one
being a boy and one being a
girl, they were as similar as Star

and Moon were different. They were twins. They both had straight dark hair, they both had thick fringes and they both had bright brown eyes. They even wore the same clothes – yellow raincoats, black jeans and blue boots.

"There he is!" Jenny said, pointing. "Isn't he gorgeous?"

"The white pony?" Jon said. "Yes, he's lovely, but I don't see what use he'd be."

"No, not the pony," Jenny said. "Look. Near him, but further down by the hedge."

Star was so wet and muddy
that it was hard to see him
against the wet bare branches
and the wet muddy grass and
the wet muddy puddles of the
field. He was sheltering, wetly
and muddily, by the hedge.

"The donkey?" Jon said. "Oh, I

see what you mean! Are we going into the yard, then, to ask? Dad said we could."

"You ask," Jenny said, suddenly nervous. "I don't want to."

"I don't want to, either," Jon said. "She might say no."

"But she might say yes," said
Jenny. "And wouldn't it be great
if . . ."

"Yes," Jon said. "Better than a
woolly lamb."

"Better than a cardboard cow,"
said Jenny.

"Better than a cut-out camel,"
said Jon.

"Much better," said Jenny. And
they looked at each other and
laughed their identical laugh.

"All right, then. We'll both ask,"
Jon decided.

And they ran together down
the drive towards the stable yard.

Chapter Four

The next afternoon, Moon's owner came to the gate with a rope halter.

"Time for you to go in," Star said to Moon, sadly. "She's early today!"

But, to his surprise, it was *his* turn to be led into the stable yard, while Moon stood puzzled by the gate.

"Come on, Star. You've got visitors," Moon's owner said to him. A boy and a girl were waiting by the gate. "Here he is. He's a bit muddy, but you can clean him up."

The twins rushed up to pat Star.

"Oh, he's *lovely*," they said.

Moon's owner fetched brushes and curry-combs, and they started to groom him, patting and stroking him all the time. Star was amazed. Surely they weren't going to take him to a donkey show? Not in the middle of winter!

They called each other Jenny and Jon, but Star couldn't see any difference between them.

While they cleaned him up, they
talked to each other in excited
voices. Jenny – or was it Jon? –
brushed out
the tassel at
the end of
Star's tail.
Jon – or was
it Jenny? – scrubbed the mud off

his hooves. Star
couldn't
remember the
last time he'd
been groomed
so carefully. If
he'd been a cat,

he would have purred to show
how much he liked it. Moon
neighed from the paddock and
trotted up and down the fence,
not used to being left out. He
didn't like it!

When the twins had brushed
off every speck of mud and
combed out every last tangle,
they led Star out of the yard and
along the lane towards the
village.

"Have I been sold?" Star wondered. "Where are they taking me? Will I ever see Moon again?"

But he wasn't going far – only to the village hall next to the

school in the main street. Star
stopped at the door, but Jenny
clicked her tongue and said,
"Come on in, Star!"

She wanted him to go right
inside the building!

Surprised, Star followed her in, walking very carefully on the wooden floor. It was Sunday today, but the village hall was full of children from the school.

The children wore strange clothes – drab draperies and droopy headdresses, or rich robes in royal colours. One little boy was carrying a toy lamb and someone else was adding the final touches to a painted cardboard cow.

A tall man and a slim lady broke away from clusters of children and came up. Their faces were amazed.

"Is this your surprise, then,
Jenny?" the man asked, stroking
Star's muzzle.

"Is this our missing ingredient,
Jon?" the lady asked, stroking
Star's ears. "Where did you find
him? He's *beautiful*!"

"Yes! This is Star," Jon said proudly.

The man turned round to the staring children.

"We have a special visitor!" he called out. "A special guest star!"

Or did he say, "A special guest, Star"?

Star was so amazed by all the attention that he couldn't be sure.

Chapter Five

Two nights later, Star waited outside the village hall for his cue. The audience waited eagerly. Every seat was taken, and some people had to stand at the sides. Star had been brushed and combed, his hooves were polished and he wore a woven cloth for a saddle. On his back sat Jenny, playing the part of Mary. By his side stood Jon, as Joseph, holding the halter rope.

They looked so different in their costumes that no-one could have guessed they were twins.

Sacking had been taped to the floorboards so that Star's hooves wouldn't slip. He had to walk the whole length of the hall to reach the painted scenery which showed the inn and the stable at Bethlehem.

"Are you ready, Star?" Jon whispered, and Jenny leaned forward to pat his neck. They were nervous, all three of them – Jon and Jenny because they had lines to remember, Star in case he tripped over the sacking, or got excited and began to bray loudly at the wrong moment.

Then Jon started to walk
forward, into the bright lights of
the hall, and Star followed. His
hooves made a muffled clopping
noise on the sackcloth. Everyone
in the audience turned and
gasped in surprise to see a real

donkey in the nativity play.

Star walked very carefully all
the way to the stage. Then Jenny
dismounted, and Jon helped her
up the steps. Star couldn't go up
the steps – all he had to do now
was wait.

But everyone was still looking at him, and people were whispering to each other and clapping. A little boy in the front row called out, "*I* want to ride that donkey, Dad!"

Star was a star!

Chapter Six

Now it's summer again. The days are long and the nights are warm. Star and Moon graze together in the paddock, side by side.

Every weekend, Moon goes off
to a show. He is washed and
plaited and groomed and taken
away in the horsebox and,
usually, he comes back with new
rosettes and trophies.

But now Star has outings too,
and needn't be envious of Moon.

He is a well-known donkey in the village now. He gets lots of invitations. He's been to the school summer fair, and next week he'll be giving rides at the village fête.

Children ride on his back and a lot of the grown-ups wish they could, too. Star behaves perfectly.

People pat him and stroke him and give him pieces of carrot and tell him how beautiful he is.

All through the summer nights, grazing under the stars, Star and Moon talk together. Moon tells Star all about the show ring, the other horses, the photographs, the prizes.

And then, when he stops talking, it's Star's turn.

THE END